VET

Rebecca Hunter

**Photography by
Chris Fairclough**

Tulip Books

www.tulipbooks.co.uk

This edition published by:
    Tulip Books
    Dept 302
    43 Owston Road
    Carcroft
    Doncaster
    DN6 8DA.

The author would like to thank Felisa Saverias and the staff and clients of the Bishopscourt Veterinary Surgery, Chelmsford, for their participation in this book.

Acknowledgements
Commissioned photography by Chris Fairclough.

Every attempt has been made by the Publisher to secure appropriate permissions for material reproduced in this book. If there has been any oversight we will be happy to rectify the situation in future editions or reprints. Written submissions should be made to the Publisher.

British Library Cataloguing in Publication Data (CIP) is available for this title.

ISBN: 978-1-78388-023-2

Printed in Spain by Edelvives

Words appearing in bold **like this**, are explained in the glossary.

Contents

I am a vet

My name is Felisa. I am a vet.

I work at the Bishopscourt Veterinary Surgery in Chelmsford, Essex. There are six vets working here.

I live just
down the road,
so I can leave
my car at home
and walk to work.

The Surgery

I arrive at the surgery at 8.30 in the morning.

I say hello to Nicola, the surgery **receptionist**.

Nicola answers the phone and makes
all the **appointments**. She tells me
which **patients** are booked in today.

The waiting room is already filling up with people and their pets.

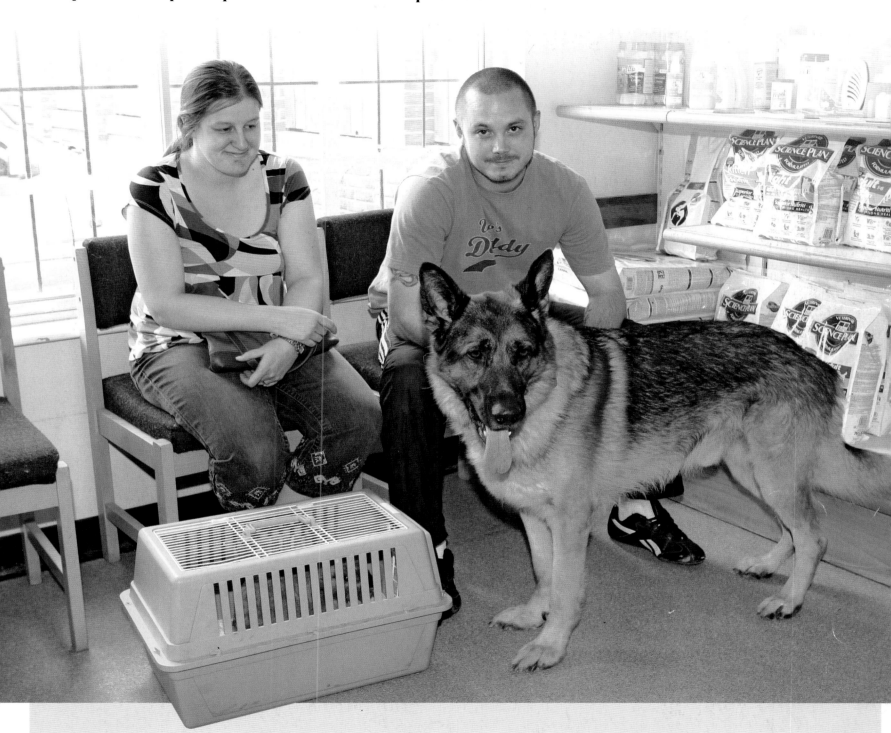

The first patient

My first patient today is a rabbit called Poppy. Emma lifts her out of her travelling box. She has brought Poppy in to have her front teeth clipped because they have grown too long.

Justine, the veterinary nurse, wraps Poppy in a towel. She holds Poppy still while I cut her teeth.

I use a pair of strong clippers. She will be able to eat more easily now.

Vaccination

This lady and her son have brought in their new kitten for a check-up and **vaccination**. The kitten is 8 weeks old and a bit scared.

First I listen to his heartbeat with my **stethoscope**.

Then I check his ears and eyes.

Then I give him the vaccination.
I tell his owners he is
very healthy but
he will need to be
treated for fleas
and to be wormed.

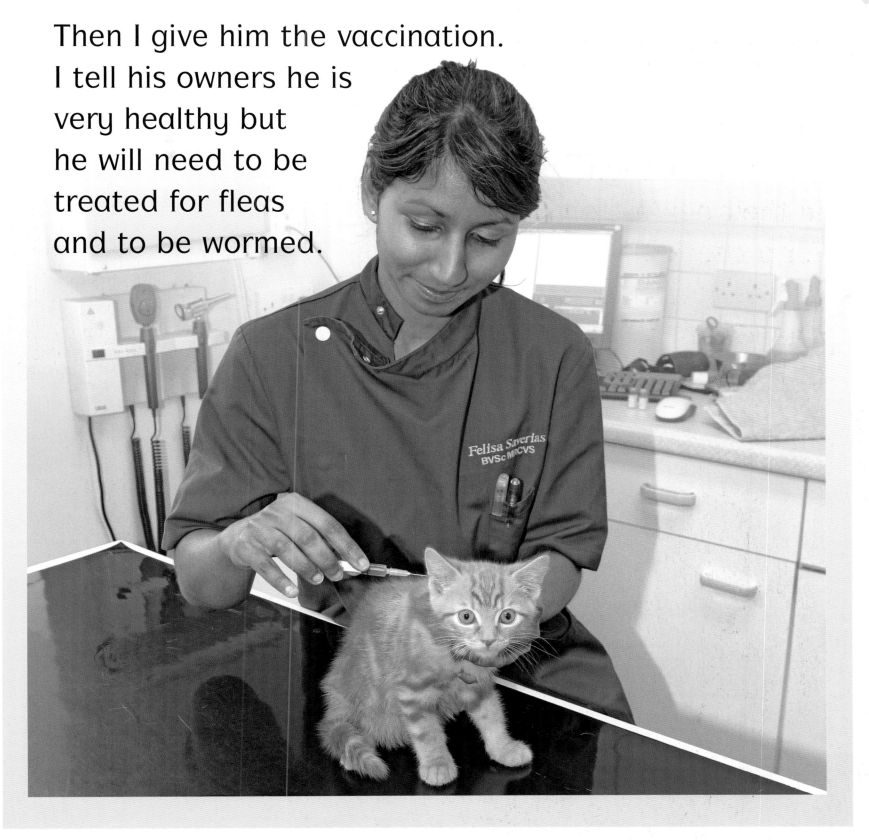

An operation

Today I am operating on a cat with an **abscess**.

We have already **anaesthetized** the cat. First I shave the area around the abscess so I can see it more clearly.

Then I wash my hands and arms. This is called scrubbing up. It is important to be very clean when you are operating.

I put on my gown, hat and gloves.

I carefully cut open the abscess with a **scalpel**. I have to scrape away the damaged **tissue** and clean the wound.

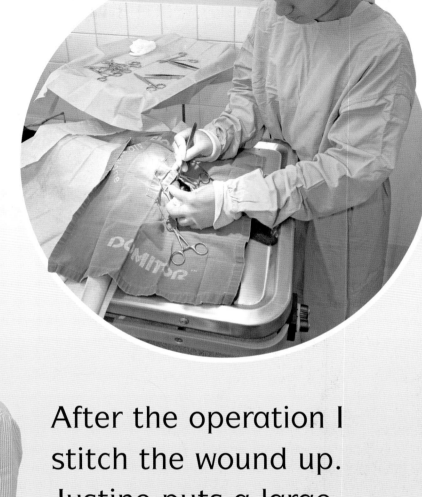

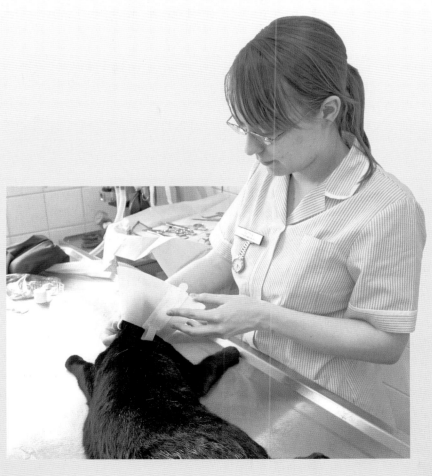

After the operation I stitch the wound up. Justine puts a large, plastic collar on the cat so it won't be able to scratch and pull out the stitches.

Lunchtime

Before I leave for lunch, I ring up the owners of the cat I operated on. I tell them that the operation went well. They can come and collect the cat this afternoon.

I go home and make myself a sandwich. It is a nice day so I eat it outside in the garden.

Then I take my dog Max for a walk.

X-rays

When I get back, Amy, one of the other vets, asks
to see me. She is treating a dog with **arthritis**. She
wants me to look at the X-ray of the dog's hips.
We discuss what treatment the dog should have.

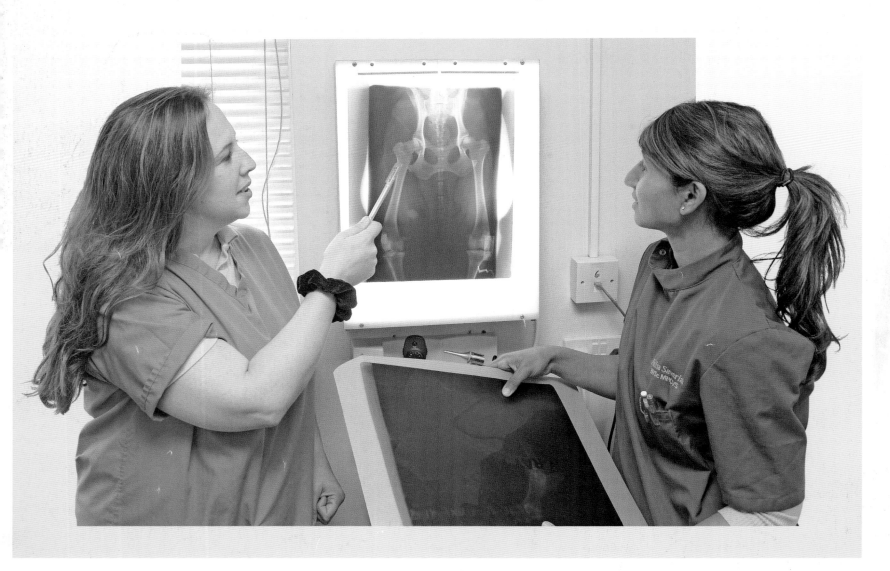

I go out to the kennels where the pets are kept when they have to stay the night with us. Tom, the **kennel hand**, is cleaning out the cages.

I help him put back the animals in their clean cages.

This dog has just woken up from its anaesthetic and it is still quite sleepy.

Microchipping

Kelly has brought her red and white setter Monty in to be **microchipped**. I inject the microchip under the skin on his neck. It doesn't hurt him – he hardly notices it.

The chip is programmed with a number. This number will go on a **National Database**. If Monty gets lost, he can be **identified** by this number and his owners can be contacted.

My next patient is a tortoise. The tortoise needs to have his toenails clipped.

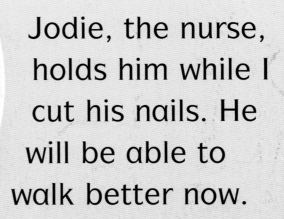

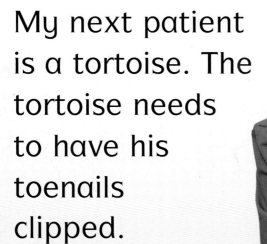

Jodie, the nurse, holds him while I cut his nails. He will be able to walk better now.

Lame cat

Julia and Lyle have a lame cat called Rosie. I think she hurt her leg in a cat fight. I examine her foot.

I take her temperature with a thermometer. It is a bit high. I will have to give her some pills.

I weigh her to see what **dosage** she should have. She weighs 4.4kg.

I go and get the pills from the **pharmacy**. This is where we keep all the medicines.

Going home

I give Julia some pills. I tell her that Rosie should have one pill a day for 3 days.

It has been another busy day but I love being a vet. Helping animals is a very rewarding job.

Glossary

abscess a swollen area filled with pus caused by a bacterial infection

anaesthetize giving a drug that causes a person or animal to go into a deep sleep

appointment an arrangement to be somewhere at a particular time

arthritis an illness that makes joints swell and ache

dosage the amount of medicine to be taken and how often

identify to recognize what something is

kennel hand a person who helps look after animals

microchip a tiny device which works like a computer

National Database a collection of information that is kept at a headquarters to be used when needed

patient a person or animal who is being given medical treatment

pharmacy a place where drugs and medicines are kept

receptionist a person who greets visitors, answers the phone and makes appointments

scalpel a very sharp knife that is used for doing operations

stethoscope a medical instrument used for listening to heartbeats and breathing

tissue the fleshy part of living things

vaccination an injection of medicine to protect a person or animal from diseases

Index